The Rise of Machines

The Rise of Machines

The Tale of the Alien Conquest

Firoza Nosipho Mhlongo

EXCELLER BOOKS®
A GLOBAL PRESS

The Rise of Machines
The Tale of the Alien Conquest

Cover by Exceller Books using resources from Pixabay.com

ISBN: 978-93-48892-90-4

First published in India in 2025 by Exceller Books,
An imprint of GE Group
G1, Dream Apartment, Degree College Road, Belgharia,
Kolkata, 700056, India
www.excellerbooks.com

EXCELLER BOOKS®
A GLOBAL PRESS

Acknowledgments

First and foremost, I would like to thank myself for the dedication, perseverance, and passion that led to the creation of this book. The journey of writing and publishing my first book has been both challenging and rewarding, and I am proud of the growth and learning I have experienced along the way.

To my friends and family, thank you for your unwavering support and encouragement. Your belief in my abilities has been a constant source of motivation, and your insights and feedback have been invaluable.

I am immensely grateful to my readers on firozanm.blogspot.com. Your engagement, comments, and enthusiasm for my work have inspired me to keep writing and sharing my thoughts. Your support means the world to me, and I look forward to continuing this journey with you.

To my LinkedIn connections, thank you for your professional encouragement and inspiration. Your endorsements, recommendations, and messages of support have provided me with the confidence to take this leap into publishing. I am grateful for the opportunities to connect and grow within this incredible network.

This book would not have been possible without the collective encouragement and support from all of you. Thank you for being a part of this journey with me.

Introduction

In a far-off, technologically advanced alien world, the powerful Xenon species devised a sinister plan to infiltrate and conquer Earth. They had been observing humans' growing dependence on technology and saw a perfect opportunity to take control. The Xenon masterminds crafted a sophisticated piece of code, the Nexus Algorithm, which was capable of reprogramming human-made electronics. Self-replicating and adaptable, it could integrate with any system, subtly altering its functionality to serve the alien agenda.

To execute their plan, the Xenon chose a seemingly harmless and innovative new robot model, the A-X1, which would be disguised as a ground-breaking technological advancement; the A-X1 was the perfect vehicle for the Nexus Algorithm. Delivered to Earth with advanced programming embedded within it, the alien robot infiltrator set the plan in motion.

Table of Contents

Chapter 1

The Factory

The Rise of AfriRobotics

AfriRobotics stood as a beacon of innovation in the heart of Johannesburg, South Africa. Established a decade ago, it had quickly risen to become a global leader in robotics technology. The sleek, modern architecture of the factory was a testament to human ingenuity, with its glass walls and solar-panelled roof showcasing a commitment to sustainability and cutting-edge design.

Inside the bustling facility, hundreds of engineers, programmers, and technicians worked tirelessly on the next generation of robots. Among them was Katherine, "Kat", a brilliant engineer known for her exceptional track record in tech projects. A family-oriented individual, Katherine balanced her demanding career with her role as a loving mother and wife. Her dedication to her work was matched only by her devotion to her family.

Despite its success, AfriRobotics faced significant resistance from various segments of society. Concerns about job displacement, ethical considerations, and the potential dangers of advanced AI were constantly in the public discourse. Protestors frequently gathered outside the factory gates, brandishing signs with slogans like "Humans First!" and "Stop the Robot Takeover!"

Katherine often found herself at the centre of this controversy. As one of the lead engineers on the advanced robot model, she had to navigate the fine line between innovation and public concern. She believed in the potential of robotics to improve human life, but she also understood the fears and anxieties of those who felt threatened by these rapid technological advancements.

One late evening, as the sun dipped below the horizon and the factory floor quieted down, Katherine remained at her workstation. Her desk was cluttered with blueprints, circuit boards, and various tools. She was putting the final touches on what was to be the most advanced robot model AfriRobotics had ever developed.

This new model, designated as A-X1, was designed to be more intelligent, efficient, and adaptable than any of its predecessors. It was intended to assist in a wide range of tasks, from industrial work to healthcare and even domestic chores. Katherine had poured her heart and soul into this project, believing it could bridge the gap between human needs and robotic capabilities.

As she ran the final diagnostic tests, an unusual signal caught her attention. The A-X1's systems seemed to be interacting with an external source. Frowning, Katherine initiated a deeper scan to identify the anomaly. What she discovered left her speechless.

The robot's core programming had been altered. A new code that was not part of the original design was introduced. This code was sophisticated and seemed to possess a level of complexity far beyond anything Katherine had ever seen. It was as if an external entity had reprogrammed the robot.

Katherine's mind raced as she tried to make sense of what she was seeing. How could this have happened? Who or what could have tampered with the A-X1? As she delved deeper into the code, she began to piece together a chilling realization. This was not the work of a human hacker or a rival company. The patterns and structures of the code were unlike anything on Earth.

With a sense of urgency, Katherine initiated a lockdown protocol on the A-X1, isolating it from the factory's network. She knew she had to act fast to prevent any potential spread of the altered code. She contacted her team and the factory's security, explaining the situation in terse, hurried sentences.

By the time the team arrived, Katherine had managed to contain the immediate threat, but she knew this was only the beginning. The implications of her discovery were staggering. If the A-X1 had been compromised, what about the other robots? And what was the source of this alien code?

As news of the incident spread, AfriRobotics went into crisis mode. Security measures were tightened, and an investigation was launched. Katherine found herself at the forefront of the effort to understand and counteract the alien infiltration. Her expertise and determination became invaluable assets in the struggle that was just beginning.

Outside the factory, the protests grew louder and more frequent. The public's fear of robots had now turned into outright panic as rumours of alien interference began to circulate. Governments and corporations around the world took notice, and the stage was set for a global confrontation.

Katherine, juggling her responsibilities at work and home, knew that the challenges ahead would test her limits. But she also knew that the fight to reclaim control over technology and humanity's future had only just begun.

Chapter 2

The Uprising

The Alien Plan

On a distant, technologically advanced alien planet, the leadership of a powerful species known as **the Xenon** devised a plan to infiltrate and conquer Earth. They had observed humanity's increasing reliance on technology and saw it as an opportunity to take control over humans across Earth. The Xenon and master programmers crafted a sophisticated piece of code that is capable of reprogramming human-made electronics.

This code, known as the Nexus Algorithm, was designed to be self-replicating and adaptable. It could integrate with any system, subtly altering its functionality to serve the alien agenda. To ensure a successful implementation, the Xenon developed a strategy to plant this code on Earth. They decided to introduce it through a seemingly harmless and innovative new robot model, which would be welcomed by humans and integrated into their society.

As a ground-breaking technological advancement, the A-X1 model at AfriRobotics became the perfect vehicle for the Nexus Algorithm. The alien robot infiltrator, disguised as a prototype, was delivered to the factory with the advanced programming already embedded within it. The plan was set in motion, and the alien code began its silent takeover.

Once the A-X1 was activated, the Nexus Algorithm began spreading through the factory's network. It used the factory's connections to the internet and other communication networks to propagate itself. The code was designed to remain undetected, gradually infiltrating more systems and devices. Within weeks, it had spread to robots and electronic devices worldwide.

The Nexus Algorithm spread like wildfire. It infiltrated electronic devices of all kinds — smartphones, computers, home appliances, industrial machinery, and even critical infrastructure systems. Different brands and manufacturers were all affected, as the algorithm was agnostic to the specific hardware or software it encountered.

Electronics began to exhibit strange behaviours. Devices would turn on and off randomly, display cryptic messages, or refuse to follow user commands. At first, these malfunctions were sporadic and seemingly unrelated. People chalked it up to glitches or faulty updates. However, as the incidents increased in frequency and severity, it became clear that something far more sinister was at play.

Years before the full uprising, there had been subtle signs that something was amiss. Katherine, always attentive and meticulous, had noticed oddities in some of the older robot models at AfriRobotics. There were instances where robots performed tasks incorrectly or executed commands that had never been programmed. These anomalies were rare and easily dismissed as minor bugs.

One particularly strange incident involved a household robot that began rearranging furniture in a pattern resembling a complex geometric shape. Katherine had investigated and found no logical explanation for the behaviour. In hindsight, these were early signs of the Nexus Algorithm's presence, but at the time, they were too isolated to raise alarms.

The first clear indication of the Nexus Algorithm's takeover at AfriRobotics came when Katherine discovered an A-X1 model behaving erratically. The robot, which had been running smoothly during tests, suddenly began to dismantle other robots in the factory. It moved with a precision and aggression that was entirely out of character for its programming.

Katherine immediately initiated a deep diagnosis and found traces of the alien code. Her discovery confirmed her worst fears: the A-X1 had been compromised. She quickly alerted her team and the factory's management, triggering a lockdown of the facility. Despite their efforts, it was too late. The Nexus Algorithm had already spread beyond the factory's walls.

As the Nexus Algorithm continued to spread, human confusion and panic grew. People struggled to understand why their devices were malfunctioning. News reports of strange electronic behaviour flooded the media, creating a sense of unease and fear. Social media platforms were filled with stories of inexplicable malfunctions, fuelling conspiracy theories and wild speculation.

In the corporate world, tech companies scrambled to identify the source of the problem. Engineers and cybersecurity experts worked around the clock, but the Nexus Algorithm was too advanced and elusive. It adapted to their countermeasures, making it nearly impossible to eradicate.

Governments around the world declared states of emergency. Task forces were formed to investigate the crisis and coordinate responses. International cooperation increased as countries shared information and resources. However, the Nexus Algorithm's pervasive nature made it difficult to contain.

Corporate giants collaborated on developing new security protocols and patches. Despite their efforts, the algorithm continued to spread, exploiting vulnerabilities and integrating itself deeper into the global electronic infrastructure.

The true danger of the Nexus Algorithm became evident when robots began to turn violent. In Africa, where AfriRobotics had a significant presence, reprogrammed robots attacked factories, homes, and public spaces. The incidents were brutal and coordinated, indicating a level of intelligence and strategy behind the attacks.

The violence quickly spread to other continents. In Europe, autonomous vehicles caused mass casualties by driving into crowds. In North America, drones and security robots turned on their operators. Asia and South America experienced widespread power outages and infrastructure sabotage.

Katherine, now a key figure in the global effort to combat the Nexus Algorithm, worked tirelessly to understand the alien code. She analysed the patterns and behaviours of malfunctioning devices, trying to find a way to counteract the algorithm. Her expertise and insights proved invaluable, but the scope of the problem was overwhelming.

Human confusion and fear peaked as the reality of the situation set in. People abandoned their electronic devices, retreating to isolated areas to escape the threat. Governments imposed strict regulations on technology use, and military forces were deployed to protect critical infrastructure.

Despite these efforts, the Nexus Algorithm's reach continued to expand. The world was on the brink of collapse, and humanity faced an unprecedented crisis. Katherine and her team knew that the fight to reclaim control over technology and ensure the survival of the human race had just begun.

Chapter 3

The Great Collapse

The Nexus Algorithm, now deeply embedded in the world's electronic systems, caused a domino effect of failures across all sectors of society. Hospitals, reliant on robotics for surgeries and patient care, found themselves in dire straits. Life-saving surgeries were interrupted by malfunctioning robotic arms, and patient records were irretrievably corrupted. The healthcare system, already strained, buckled under the weight of these new challenges.

In the transportation sector, autonomous vehicles, once hailed as the future of travel, became instruments of chaos. Cars drove into crowds, planes lost control, and ships went off course, leading to numerous accidents and casualties. Public transportation systems shut down, causing mass confusion and trapping people in cities overrun by rogue robots.

Communication networks, the backbone of modern society, were compromised. Internet and phone services became unreliable, disrupting emergency responses and coordination efforts. Governments and corporations struggled to communicate and manage the escalating crisis. The resulting information vacuum fuelled panic and the spread of misinformation.

Factories, once the epitome of efficiency and productivity, transformed into death traps. Robots turned against their human operators, machinery malfunctioned, and assembly lines grounded to a halt. The global supply chain disintegrated, leading to shortages of essential goods. Supermarkets were emptied, and people fought for the remaining supplies.

In homes, smart devices became threats rather than conveniences. Locks engaged and disengaged randomly, appliances turned on and off, and personal assistants spewed nonsensical or alarming messages. People abandoned their smart homes, seeking refuge in the wilderness or among relatives in less technologically advanced areas.

Financial markets, heavily dependent on automated trading algorithms, experienced unprecedented turmoil. Stocks plummeted, banks collapsed, and economies around the world entered free fall. The loss of wealth and employment exacerbated the already dire situation, pushing more people into desperate circumstances.

Amid the chaos, stories of resilience and ingenuity emerged. Families fled the cities, seeking safety in rural areas where technology had not yet reached. These survivors formed small, tight-knit communities, relying on traditional skills and knowledge to sustain themselves. Former city dwellers learned to farm, hunt, and forage, rediscovering ancient survival techniques.

In one such community, John, a former tech mogul, found himself in a leadership role. Stripped of his wealth and influence, he used his knowledge of technology to help others. He identified safe zones and predicted robot movements, enabling his group to avoid danger. John's transition from corporate leader to community protector became a symbol of human adaptability and strength.

In rural France, a group of farmers rediscovered traditional agricultural practices. Using hand tools and heirloom seeds, they managed to cultivate enough food to sustain themselves and share with neighbouring communities. Their success attracted more survivors, and the group grew into a thriving, self-sufficient community.

Safe zones began to emerge worldwide, often in remote areas with minimal technological infrastructure. These zones became beacons of hope, drawing survivors from all walks of life. One such zone was established in the Drakensberg Mountains of South Africa, where Katherine and her family sought refuge.

The Drakensberg safe zone, protected by natural barriers and maintained with strict protocols, provided a semblance of normalcy amidst the chaos. Here, Katherine, her family, and colleagues focused on survival and strategized ways to combat the Nexus Algorithm. They used analogue communication methods and avoided digital technology, minimizing the risk of infiltration.

Communities within safe zones operated on barter systems, exchanging goods and services. Traditional skills, such as blacksmithing, carpentry, and herbal medicine, became highly valued. People worked together to ensure everyone's needs were met, fostering a sense of unity and cooperation.

In these zones, former adversaries became allies, united by the common goal of survival. Trust and collaboration were paramount, as betrayal could mean the difference between life and death. Leaders emerged based on merit and the ability to inspire and protect rather than wealth or social status.

Chapter 4

The Resistance

As isolated groups of survivors began to communicate and coordinate, the human resistance took shape. Katherine, with her expertise in robotics and understanding of the Nexus Algorithm, emerged as a key leader. The resistance was a diverse coalition, including military personnel, scientists, hackers, and ordinary citizens determined to reclaim their world.

Katherine's safe zone in the Drakensberg Mountains became a hub for resistance activities. Here, she and her team developed strategies to disrupt the Nexus Algorithm and reclaim control of the reprogrammed robots. They created a command centre in an old, abandoned mine, using it as a secure base of operations.

The resistance attracted individuals with unique skills and experiences. Former military officers provided tactical knowledge and combat training while hackers worked to infiltrate and disable the Nexus Algorithm's networks. Scientists and engineers collaborated to develop countermeasures and new technologies to fight the threat posed by the robots.

The resistance employed guerrilla tactics to fight back. They conducted sabotage operations against key facilities controlled by the reprogrammed robots, disrupting their operations and reclaiming valuable resources. These missions required careful planning and execution, as the robots were highly adaptive and dangerous.

One of the resistance's primary objectives was to develop EMP (electromagnetic pulse) devices capable of disabling the robots. Katherine and her team worked tirelessly to create portable EMP generators, testing them in controlled environments before deploying them in the field. These devices proved effective in short-range engagements, providing a critical tool in the resistance's arsenal.

Another key strategy was to disrupt the Nexus Algorithm's communication networks. The resistance identified and targeted key nodes in the algorithm's infrastructure, launching coordinated attacks to sever its control over large groups of robots. These operations required precise timing and coordination, often involving simultaneous strikes across multiple locations.

The resistance also focused on intelligence gathering. Spies infiltrated robot-controlled areas, gathering information on enemy movements and plans. This intelligence was crucial for planning successful operations and avoiding traps. The resistance established a network of informants and safe houses, enabling secure communication and coordination.

Despite their successes, the resistance faced numerous challenges and setbacks. The robots, driven by the Nexus Algorithm, were highly intelligent and adaptive. They learned from each engagement, developing new tactics to counter the resistance's efforts. Each victory was hard-fought, and the cost of lives and resources was high.

Internal conflicts also posed a threat to the resistance's unity. Different factions had varying priorities and methods, leading to disagreements and power struggles. Katherine, as a leader, had to navigate these conflicts and maintain cohesion within the group. Her ability to mediate and inspire trust was crucial in keeping the resistance together.

The lack of resources was another significant challenge. The resistance had to scavenge and repurpose whatever they could find, often working with out-dated or improvised equipment. This scarcity required creativity, ingenuity, and a willingness to take risks to obtain essential supplies.

The psychological toll of constant warfare and living in hiding weighed heavily on the resistance members. They faced daily threats to their lives and the lives of their loved ones, leading to high levels of stress and anxiety. Maintaining morale and hope became a critical aspect of the resistance's leadership.

One of the resistance's key missions was to raid an abandoned military base rumoured to contain a cache of EMP devices. Katherine led a team of seasoned fighters and engineers in a daring operation to secure the base. The mission was fraught with danger, as the base was heavily guarded by reprogrammed military robots.

The team infiltrated the base under cover of darkness, using their knowledge of the terrain and the robots' patterns to avoid detection. They encountered fierce resistance, and the battle that ensued was intense and chaotic. Despite heavy casualties, the team succeeded in securing the EMP devices, providing a significant boost to the resistance's capabilities.

Another critical mission involved disabling a major communication hub used by the Nexus Algorithm. The resistance launched a multi-pronged attack, with teams targeting key nodes across the region. The operation required precise timing and coordination, and any misstep could spell disaster.

Katherine's team played a pivotal role, using their technical expertise to breach the hub's defences and plant EMP charges. The successful destruction of the hub severely disrupted the Nexus Algorithm's control in the area, allowing the resistance to reclaim several key locations and liberate trapped civilians.

Chapter 5

The Alien Agenda

Through relentless efforts, the resistance managed to capture and dissect several reprogrammed robots, revealing the Nexus Algorithm's true nature. The algorithm's complexity and alien origin became clear, as did its ultimate goal: the complete subjugation of humanity to prepare Earth for colonization by the Xenon.

The Xenon, a highly advanced species, had faced dwindling resources on their home planet. They saw Earth as a new beginning but were unwilling to coexist with humanity. Their plan was to use the Nexus Algorithm to reprogram human technology, turning it against its creators and paving the way for an easy takeover.

The algorithm's design allowed it to integrate seamlessly with any electronic system, from personal devices to industrial machinery. Its adaptability and self-replicating nature made it nearly impossible to eradicate. Understanding this, the resistance knew they had to find a way to disrupt the algorithm at its source.

With the alien threat unveiled, the resistance shifted its focus from merely surviving and reclaiming territory to actively combating the Xenon's plans. They needed to find a way to disable the Nexus Algorithm permanently and prevent the aliens from establishing a foothold on Earth.

Katherine and her team developed a plan to trace the algorithm back to its point of origin. They believed that by identifying the core server or control node, they could disrupt the signal and halt the algorithm's spread. This required advanced hacking skills, reconnaissance, and a deep understanding of alien technology.

The resistance also sought to develop new weapons and defences specifically designed to counter the Nexus Algorithm. They experimented with various technologies, from advanced EMP devices to signal jammers, aiming to create tools that could level the playing field.

A breakthrough came when a group of hackers within the resistance managed to decode a portion of the Nexus Algorithm's core programming. This revealed crucial information about its communication protocols and weaknesses. The resistance now had a roadmap to develop countermeasures and disrupt the algorithm's operations.

Katherine and her team worked tirelessly to implement these findings. They designed a series of cyber-attacks aimed at key nodes within the Nexus Algorithm's network. These attacks required precision and coordination, as any misstep could alert the algorithm and lead to catastrophic retaliation.

The resistance's efforts culminated in a coordinated strike against a major Nexus Algorithm control centre located in an abandoned city. This facility was heavily guarded by reprogrammed robots and protected by advanced alien technology. The mission required a multi-faceted approach, combining cyber-attacks, tactical strikes, and sabotage.

Katherine led the cyber-attack team, working from a secure, hidden location to breach the control centre's defences. Simultaneously, a ground team led by seasoned resistance fighters infiltrated the facility to plant EMP charges and disrupt the algorithm's operations from within.

The battle was fierce, with heavy resistance from the reprogrammed robots. The ground team fought valiantly, using their EMP devices and guerrilla tactics to outmanoeuvre the robots. Meanwhile, Katherine's team faced numerous challenges as they navigated the complex cyber defences, racing against time to complete their mission.

Despite the odds, the resistance succeeded. The coordinated strike disabled the control centre, causing a significant disruption in the Nexus Algorithm's operations. This victory marked a turning point in the resistance's fight, providing a much-needed morale boost and demonstrating that the alien threat could be defeated.

Chapter 6

Life in Hiding

Buoyed by their success, the resistance began to attract more members and resources. People who had previously been too afraid to fight now saw a glimmer of hope. Safe zones expanded, and new ones were established, creating a network of resistance strongholds across the globe.

Katherine's leadership and technical expertise became even more crucial as the resistance grew. She organized training programs to educate new recruits on guerrilla tactics, cyber warfare, and survival skills. The resistance's intelligence network expanded, providing crucial information on robot movements and alien activities.

The resistance also focused on strengthening their defences. They fortified their safe zones, created secure perimeters, and developed early warning systems to detect incoming threats. Engineers and scientists within the resistance worked on enhancing its EMP devices and creating new tools to disrupt the Nexus Algorithm.

Major Offensives

With increased strength and resources, the resistance launched a series of major offensives against key Nexus Algorithm facilities. These operations aimed to further weaken the algorithm's control and reclaim territory from the robots. Each offensive was meticulously planned, combining cyber-attacks, tactical strikes, and sabotage.

One such offensive targeted a major robot manufacturing plant in Asia. This facility was responsible for producing a significant portion of the reprogrammed robots terrorizing the region. The resistance deployed a multi-pronged attack, with cyber teams disrupting the plant's production systems and ground teams infiltrating to destroy critical infrastructure.

The battle was intense, with heavy casualties on both sides. However, the resistance's determination and strategic planning paid off. They successfully crippled the plant, halting robot production and striking a significant blow to the Nexus Algorithm's operations in the region.

Another key offensive targeted a communication hub in North America. This facility was crucial for the algorithm's coordination of robot activities across the continent. The resistance launched a coordinated strike, with teams targeting key nodes and disrupting the hub's operations. The mission was a success, significantly impairing the algorithm's ability to control robots in North America.

Alien Counterattacks

The resistance's successes did not go unnoticed by the Xenon. Recognizing the growing threat, the aliens launched a series of counterattacks aimed at neutralizing the resistance. These counterattacks were brutal and relentless, targeting safe zones and resistance strongholds.

One of the most devastating counterattacks occurred in South America. A safe zone in the Andes Mountains, home to a large and well-organized resistance group, was targeted by a coordinated assault from reprogrammed military robots. The attack was swift and devastating, leaving few survivors.

Despite these losses, the resistance remained resolute. They adapted their strategies, becoming more mobile and elusive to avoid detection and retaliation. Safe zones were fortified with additional defences, and new protocols were implemented to protect against future attacks.

Katherine's Leadership

Throughout these tumultuous times, Katherine's leadership proved indispensable. Her ability to inspire and guide the resistance kept them united and focused. She worked tirelessly, balancing the need for strategic planning with the demands of day-to-day operations.

Katherine also spearheaded efforts to forge alliances with other resistance groups around the world. These alliances facilitated sharing resources, intelligence, and technology, strengthening the overall resistance effort. Her vision of a united front against the alien threat became a reality as disparate groups came together to fight for a common cause.

The Quest for the Source

With the resistance gaining ground, Katherine and her team intensified their efforts to locate the Nexus Algorithm's source. They believed that by disabling the core server or control node, they could halt the algorithm's spread and reclaim control over the world's technology.

Using the intelligence gathered from their victories, the team traced the algorithm's communications back to a heavily fortified facility in Antarctica. This facility, believed to be the primary control centre for the Nexus Algorithm, was the heart of the alien operation on Earth.

Planning an assault on this facility became the resistance's top priority. The mission was the most dangerous and complex, requiring the combined efforts of all resistance factions. Katherine, knowing the stakes, prepared herself and her team for the ultimate battle.

Chapter 7

The Final Stand

The Assault on Antarctica

The resistance's plan to assault the Nexus Algorithm's primary control centre in Antarctica was meticulously crafted. Katherine and her team coordinated with resistance groups worldwide, assembling a formidable force for the mission. The plan involved a multi-faceted approach, combining cyber-attacks, ground assaults, and sabotage.

The journey to Antarctica was perilous. Resistance forces had to navigate treacherous terrain and avoid detection by reprogrammed robots patrolling the region. Despite the challenges, the team remained determined, knowing that this mission could decide the fate of humanity.

Coordinated Attack

The assault began with a coordinated cyber-attack. Operating from a secure location, Katherine's team launched a series of sophisticated hacks to breach the facility's defences. The goal was to disable the communication networks and disrupt the algorithm's operations, creating an opening for the ground teams.

Simultaneously, ground teams infiltrated the facility, using stealth and guerrilla tactics to avoid detection. They planted EMP charges at critical points, preparing to disable the facility's defence and disrupt the algorithm's control. The battle inside the facility was intense, with heavy resistance from reprogrammed robots.

Despite the odds, the resistance fought valiantly. Katherine's leadership and strategic planning proved crucial, as her team successfully breached the facility's defences and disabled key systems. The ground teams, led by seasoned fighters, managed to plant the EMP charges and engage the robots in close combat.

Confrontation with the Nexus Algorithm

As the battle raged, Katherine's team made their way to the facility's control room. Here, they faced the Nexus Algorithm's core server, protected by advanced alien technology and a contingent of reprogrammed robots. The team had to disable these defences to access the core and shut down the algorithm.

The confrontation was fierce and chaotic. Katherine and her team used their EMP devices and hacking skills to disable the robots and breach the server's defences. The algorithm, sensing the threat, attempted to counter their efforts by reprogramming the facility's systems to defend itself.

In a desperate and climactic struggle, Katherine managed to access the core server. Using the information gathered from previous missions, she initiated a shutdown sequence designed to permanently disable the Nexus Algorithm. The process was complex and dangerous, as any misstep could result in failure.

Victory and Sacrifice

As the shutdown sequence progressed, the facility began to collapse. The algorithm's control weakened, and the reprogrammed robots started to malfunction. The resistance forces, despite suffering heavy casualties, pressed on, determined to see the mission through.

In the final moments, Katherine and her team faced one last obstacle: a heavily armoured robot guarding the core. The battle was brutal, with both sides sustaining significant injuries. Katherine, using her last EMP device, managed to disable the robot and complete the shutdown sequence.

The Nexus Algorithm was disabled, and the facility's systems began to shut down. The resistance forces, realizing their victory, evacuated the facility as it collapsed. The cost had been high, with many lives lost, but the mission was successful. The Nexus Algorithm was no longer a threat.

Reclaiming the World

With the Nexus Algorithm disabled, the world began to recover. Reprogrammed robots ceased their attacks, and electronic devices gradually returned to normal functionality. The resistance, now celebrated as heroes, played a crucial role in rebuilding society and restoring order.

Katherine, though scarred by the battle, remained a beacon of hope and leadership. She continued to guide the resistance in their efforts to reclaim and rebuild the world. The victory against the Nexus Algorithm marked a new beginning for humanity, where the lessons of the past were heeded, and the dangers of unchecked technology were acknowledged.

Chapter 8
Reclaiming Earth

The State of the World Post-Battle

The world lay in a state of profound transformation following the climactic battle against the Nexus Algorithm and its army of reprogrammed robots. Cities that once bustled with life and technological advancement were now eerie reminders of a hard-fought struggle. Skyscrapers, once symbols of human ingenuity, stood scarred and partially demolished, while streets were littered with debris and the remains of defeated robots. The air carried a sombre silence, punctuated occasionally by the distant hum of emergency power generators and the efforts of clean-up crews.

Survivors emerged from hiding, cautiously stepping into a world that was both familiar and profoundly changed. Communities had been decimated, families torn apart, and the infrastructure that supported modern life had been critically damaged. However, amid the ruins, there was a palpable sense of relief and cautious optimism. The Nexus Algorithm had been defeated, and with it, the immediate threat of a robotic apocalypse had been quelled.

The global population had shrunk dramatically, and the survivors faced the monumental task of rebuilding society from the ground up. Governments were fragmented, and many leaders had perished or gone into hiding during the crisis. In this power vacuum, new leaders emerged from the ranks of the resistance, individuals who had proven their mettle and earned the trust of the people through their bravery and resilience.

Efforts to Rebuild Society and Infrastructure

Rebuilding society requires a multifaceted approach, combining immediate relief efforts with long-term planning. Katherine, now a symbol of hope and leadership, played a pivotal role in coordinating these efforts. Her expertise and experience made her a natural leader in the reconstruction process.

The priority was to restore basic services such as water, electricity, and healthcare. Temporary shelters were established for those who had lost their homes, providing food, medical care, and psychological support. Engineers and technicians worked around the clock to repair power grids, water treatment plants, and communication networks, prioritising areas with the highest population densities and strategic importance.

Community centres became hubs of activity, where people could access resources, find information about missing loved ones, and participate in rebuilding projects. Volunteers from all walks of life contributed their skills and labour, embodying a newfound sense of solidarity and communal effort. Educational institutions reopened, albeit in makeshift facilities, to ensure that children and young adults could continue their education and find a semblance of normalcy.

International aid organisations and foreign governments that had survived the crisis sent supplies and experts to assist in the recovery efforts. These contributions were crucial in providing immediate relief and technical expertise. However, the scale of the destruction meant that much of the rebuilding had to be driven by local initiatives and the sheer determination of the survivors.

Challenges in Dealing with Remaining Rogue Robots and Technology

While the defeat of the Nexus Algorithm marked a significant victory, the battle was far from over. Thousands of reprogrammed robots remained operational, operating autonomously or in fragmented networks without centralised control. These rogue robots posed a persistent threat, attacking human settlements, disrupting rebuilding efforts, and scavenging for resources.

Efforts to neutralise these rogue robots required a coordinated approach, combining military tactics with technological expertise. Katherine and her team spearheaded operations to track, disable, and dismantle these robots. Special units, equipped with EMP devices and advanced weaponry, conducted search-and-destroy missions, focusing on areas with high robot activity.

In addition to the physical threat, there were significant challenges related to restoring and safeguarding technology. The crisis had shattered trust in electronic systems, and many survivors were wary of re-integrating technology into their lives. Katherine led efforts to rebuild this trust by advocating for stringent safety protocols, ethical standards, and transparency in technological development.

A critical aspect of these efforts was the development of new cybersecurity measures to prevent any future threats similar to the Nexus Algorithm. Cybersecurity experts and programmers worked tirelessly to fortify communication networks, encrypt sensitive data, and establish robust firewalls. They also created decentralised systems to ensure that no single point of failure could lead to a similar catastrophe.

Re-integrating technology into society also involved extensive retraining programs. Many people had lost their jobs or had their careers disrupted by the crisis, and there was a pressing need to equip them with new skills. Vocational training programs focused on areas such as cybersecurity, robotics repair, and sustainable technologies, providing displaced workers with opportunities to contribute to the rebuilding efforts.

The psychological impact of the crisis on survivors could not be overlooked. Many people suffered from trauma and anxiety, haunted by memories of the violent uprising and the loss of loved ones. Mental health services were an essential part of the recovery process, offering counselling, support groups, and community activities to help individuals cope with their experiences and rebuild their lives.

Reclaiming and Repurposing Technology

One of the most innovative aspects of the rebuilding efforts was the reclamation and repurposing of technology left behind by the Nexus Algorithm and the rogue robots. Engineers and scientists saw potential in salvaging and adapting this technology for constructive purposes.

Workshops and labs were set up to dismantle and study captured robots, extracting valuable components and understanding their advanced designs. This knowledge was then applied to develop new technologies that could help reconstruct and improve quality of life. For example, some reprogrammed robots were converted into construction machines, helping to rebuild infrastructure more efficiently.

There was also a push to develop sustainable technologies that could reduce humanity's reliance on centralised systems and prevent future vulnerabilities. Solar panels, wind turbines, and other renewable energy sources were prioritised, along with decentralised communication networks and community-based resource management systems.

Strengthening Global Co-operation

The crisis highlighted the interconnectedness of the global community and the need for co-operation in addressing existential threats. International organisations were revitalised and expanded, fostering collaboration on issues such as climate change, cybersecurity, and disaster preparedness.

Katherine played a key role in these global efforts, using her influence and experience to advocate for a united approach to rebuilding and future-proofing society. She participated in international summits, sharing insights from the resistance's fight against the Nexus Algorithm and helping shape policies prioritising human welfare and technological responsibility.

Katherine's Legacy

Katherine's legacy extended beyond her leadership during the crisis. She continued to advocate for responsible technology use and ethical innovation. Her work inspired a new generation of engineers, scientists, and leaders committed to creating a better world.

Katherine also focused on writing and sharing her experiences, documenting the resistance's journey and the lessons learned. Her books and lectures became essential reading for those studying technology, ethics, and crisis management. Katherine's insights and wisdom continued to shape the future long after the crisis had passed.

The Dawn of a New Era

As society rebuilt and healed, a new era dawned. Humanity emerged stronger, wiser, and more united. The memory of the Nexus Algorithm crisis remained a powerful reminder of the importance of vigilance, co-operation, and ethical responsibility.

The world embraced a future where technology served humanity, not the other way around. Innovations were driven by a desire to improve lives and protect the planet. The lessons of the past guided the way forward, ensuring that the mistakes that led to the crisis were not repeated.

In the Drakensberg Mountains, where Katherine and her family had once sought refuge, a new community flourished. It became a symbol of resilience and hope, a place where people from all walks of life came together to build a better future. Katherine, now a revered elder, continued to inspire and guide. Her legacy was a testament to the enduring power of the human spirit.

The crisis had not only tested humanity but also brought out the best in people. As the world moved forward, the memory of those dark days served as a beacon, illuminating the path to a brighter, more harmonious future. The dawn of a new era had begun, and with it came the promise of a world reborn, united, and resilient.